Parker's Pumpkin

written by Jean Huxtable-Hamersky
& Jack Hamersky

Illustrated by Jeanna Krause

"As a school principal, I always searched for enjoyable read-aloud books to share with classrooms. This book would be on my list . . . a must-read for children!"

– *Lois A. Cuff; retired elementary educator, principal, and superintendent*

"*Parker's Pumpkin* is a wonderful example of embracing children's natural curiosity. The relationship between Parker and his grandmother cultivates a fun and natural environment for learning."

–*Bethany Barnes, elementary educator*

"*Parker's Pumpkin* should be part of a science unit in every elementary school. The book is rich in ideas for students to explore, including composting, pollinators, growing garden plants indoors, and how flowers give us fruit. *Parker's Pumpkin* also teaches essential elements of science: wonder, curiosity, and creativity."

–*Steve Bennett, Ph.D.; K-16 science education researcher at Michigan State University*

Published by Orange Hat Publishing 2023
PB ISBN: 9781645387237
HC ISBN: 9781645387220

Copyrighted © 2023 by Jean Huxtable-Hamersky & Jack Hamersky
All Rights Reserved
Parker's Pumpkin
Written by Jean Huxtable-Hamersky & Jack Hamersky
Illustrated by Jeanna Krause

This publication and all contents within may not be reproduced or transmitted in any part or in its entirety without the written permission of the author.

orangehatpublishing.com

For Parker—his curiosity and love of gardens, insects, mushrooms, octopuses, volcanos, and everything in the great outdoors.

"Grandma, where are you?" Parker yelled, as he rode his bike up to Grandma's house. He was always excited to go to Grandma's house because she was always getting into adventures, and her house and yard were full of lots of interesting gadgets, contraptions, and garden experiments. Much different from the plain houses next door.

"I'm out in the garden, honey," Grandma replied.

"Which one?" yelled Parker again.

Parker found Grandma in the backyard veggie garden, holding up a big seed.

"Look what I found!" exclaimed Grandma. "It was up in the attic, inside a dusty old trunk. And it was folded up inside a page from an old calendar..."

"It looks like a pumpkin seed, but it's really big. Let's plant it and see what happens!" Parker said.

Parker and Grandma filled a pot with potting soil. Then Parker put the seed down into the soil, carefully covered it with a little more, and sprinkled it with some water.

"Let's find a sunny spot for it to warm up and see if it sprouts," Parker said.

Each day, Parker returned to Grandma's house to check on the seed, and on the fifth day, he saw a little sprout poking out of the soil. "This thing is growing fast!" Parker said as they stared at the pot in amazement.

Then they heard a pop and saw another leaf sprout. Grandma and he looked at each other with startled eyes.

"I didn't think it could grow this fast!" Parker said.

"I don't know," said Grandma. "We might have bitten off more than we can chew!"

Each day, the sprout grew bigger and bigger, until after a couple weeks, the vine was as long as Parker's bike. He and Grandma had to put it into a bigger pot.

As the days went by, the vine grew longer and longer. But the weather got colder, and Grandma and Parker worried that the cold weather would kill the vine.

So one day, they decided to bring the pot and the long vine into Grandma's house. They put it in front of a large window, where the vine would have lots of sunshine.

Grandma and Parker watered the plant every few days, and the vine continued to grow and wind its way through the living room.

It kept growing and growing, through the house and out the chimney and back through a window until it filled most of Grandma's house. It filled the house so much that Parker had a hard time finding Grandma and her puppy when he visited.

One day, behind a leaf they found a big, bright orange flower blooming on the vine. "I know what those are, Grandma. Those turn into pumpkins."

And sure enough, within a couple days, a little, round orange pumpkin had formed where the blossom had been.

Parker and Grandma watched as the pumpkin grew and grew and grew. It grew so fast that furniture had to be moved.

The next week, it had grown so big that they needed to put wood down and reinforce the flooring under the pumpkin so it wouldn't fall through the floor! The pumpkin got so big, they began to worry about how they would get the pumpkin out of the house.

Parker called his friends and said, "You have to come and see this pumpkin." People began hearing about the pumpkin, and they investigated, coming by and peeking through the window. The whole town was talking about how to get the pumpkin out of the house.

"We might have to remove the roof!" said Parker one day.

"No," said Grandma, "I have an idea. Let's have a pumpkin pie feast!"

So, Parker made signs and hung them all over town.

The day finally came to harvest the pumpkin, and Parker rode to his grandma's house to find people lined up and down the street.

"Are you ready, Grandma?" asked Parker.

"You bet," said Grandma.

The two of them climbed their ladders to the top of the pumpkin and began to cut with a two-person lumberjack saw. People lined up at the window to get their piece of pumpkin, and they carried it home to make pumpkin pies.

On the day of the feast, tables lined the streets with all the pumpkin pies you could eat! People came from miles around. The newspaper and TV station showed up to take pictures.

It took days to clean up and put the vine and all the leftover pumpkin in the garden compost.

Winter came to the town, and everyone talked about Parker's giant pumpkin and all the fun they'd had at the pumpkin feast.

Spring came afterward, and one day Parker got a call from his grandma.

"I have a surprise for you," she said. "Can you come over?"

PUMPKIN FACTS

A pumpkin weigh-off is a competition where pumpkin growers bring their gigantic pumpkins to be weighed and measured. Each state has their own weigh-offs in the fall. Many competitions offer prize money for the biggest and heaviest pumpkins. A special scale is used to weigh giant pumpkins at weigh-offs. Forklifts and cranes lift these pumpkins onto a huge scale.

The best way to obtain seeds to grow a giant pumpkin is to ask a competitive grower. They will know the genetic potential of each of their seeds for a record-sized giant pumpkin.

Before you plant your giant pumpkin seed, lightly sand the edges (except the pointy end) and soak your seed in warm water for 60 minutes. Squeeze out any water and plant in warm soil with the pointy end down.

Once they sprout, pumpkins take between 90–130 days to reach maturity, so start your seeds indoors in April or May, or outdoors if the weather is 70–90 degrees (Fahrenheit).

Giant pumpkins require lots of sunshine and moist, well-drained soil that is organically rich. Pumpkins are 80-90% water, so water them regularly. Giant pumpkins can soak up to 100 gallons of water per day.

A giant pumpkin needs about 300 square feet to grow.

The biggest pumpkin grown in the United States was grown in 2022 and weighed 2,554 pounds.

There are over 250 types of pumpkins grown in North America.

To grow a Halloween pumpkin, you should start between May and June.

www.bigpumpkins.com
https://www.youtube.com/watch?v=9hpxXddu3aU
https://www.youtube.com/watch?v=W4ExVFLPftw
Mark Clementz on YouTube

A compost pile can simply be a place about three feet in diameter in your yard surrounded by a low fence, or it can be enclosed in a bin (which you can purchase at your local garden store). Compost piles are composed of layers of shredded cardboard or newspaper and green materials like grass clippings, leaves, and vegetable and fruit peelings and cores. Add water and mix the layers with a shovel. Eventually, when your compost looks like soil, it is ready to use to enrich the soil in your garden.

Pumpkins are packed with lots of good nutrients. They are low in calories, rich in antioxidants, and rich in Vitamin C and potassium.

Many good foods can be made with pumpkins: pies, cakes, muffins, cookies, soups and stews, roasted seeds, cheesecakes, salads, and lattes. Pumpkin flowers can be fried or used in salads.

Although many people think of pumpkins as vegetables, they are actually a fruit (because they develop from a flower).

Pumpkin vines contain both male and female flowers. The female pumpkin flower only opens for a day for pollination.

Once the flowers bloom and pumpkins are growing on the vine, choose the one you want to grow and remove the others. This sends the nutrients into that one pumpkin.

To grow giant pumpkins, the weather needs to be sunny and warm during the day, and the temperature cannot be lower than 65 degrees at night.

Extra pumpkins can be donated to zoos or farmers to feed pigs and cattle or used as fertilizer on their fields. They can also be added to a compost pile to enrich gardens or shared with those who do not have pumpkins.

Pumpkins come in many sizes and can be bumpy or smooth on the outside. They can be short, tall, flat, or wide.

The best pumpkins for carving usually weigh between 10-12 pounds. Small pumpkins are best for eating and are known as "Pumpkin Pie Pumpkins."

Pumpkins can be dark green, orange, yellow, or white.

The flesh of some pumpkins can be a bright orange color, blue, or white.

Parker's Pumpkin Pie

Mix together:
1 cup sugar, 1 tablespoon flour, ¼ teaspoon salt, and 1 tablespoon cinnamon.

Add: 1 ½ cup pumpkin, 1 large egg, 1 cup milk. Mix until it looks creamy like pudding.

Pour into a pie crust and bake at 425 degrees for 45-55 minutes.

Don't forget to cover the edges of the crust with foil so they don't get too brown.

About the Authors

Jean Huxtable-Hamersky has always loved being outside in the natural world, growing plants, gardening, hiking, and exploring. This story is based partly on a gardening adventure that she had with her nine-year-old grandson, Parker. Jean was born and raised in Nebraska, graduated from University of Nebraska-Lincoln, and spent forty-five years working as a speech-language pathologist with preschoolers. She is retired now and has lived and adventured in Upper Michigan and Wisconsin (in the Great Lakes area) for the past thirty-five years.

Jack Hamersky grew up in Northeast Wisconsin, where he learned the joy of observing the changes of nature and the seasons. Outdoor activities were commonplace in his childhood, whether it was fishing, maple syruping, or gardening. As a child, planting a seed always filled him with the excitement of what could be. He now lives in Alabama and hopes to pass down his love for gardening and the outdoors to his children.

About the Illustrator

Jeanna Krause is an illustrator from rural Wisconsin who grew up enjoying the beauty of rolling fields, bluffs, and cold rivers. Her love of nature always finds a way into her artwork, and she hopes to inspire joy in others, young and old alike, with whimsical and bright paintings. You can find her on Instagram @JeannaCreates.

Printed in the USA
CPSIA information can be obtained
at www.ICGtesting.com
LVHW070607081024
792933LV00048B/162